The Alligator with the Lean Mean Smile

The Alligator with the Lean Mean Smile

by Lillian Nordlicht

illustrated by Dennis Hockerman

SCHOLASTIC INC.

NEW YORK • TORONTO • LONDON • AUCKLAND • SYDNEY

Scholastic Canada Ltd.
123 Newkirk Road, Richmond Hill, Ontario, Canada L4C 3G5

Scholastic Inc.
730 Broadway, New York, NY 10003, USA

Ashton Scholastic Limited
Private Bag 1, Penrose, Auckland, New Zealand

Ashton Scholastic Pty Limited
PO Box 579, Gosford, NSW 2250, Australia

Scholastic Publications Ltd.
Holly Walk, Leamington Spa, Warwickshire CV32 4LS, England

ISBN 0-590-41362-7

7 6 5 4 3 2   Printed in Canada   1 2 3 4 5 / 9

To my three sons:
Robert, Scott, and Jonathan

Small Hippo
and Big Rhino
lived deep in the forest.

They took
long walks to the river.
They liked to sit
in the water
and splash each other.

One day a stranger
poked his head
above the water.

"Who are you?"
asked Small Hippo.

"And what are you doing here?"
asked Big Rhino.

The alligator didn't answer.
Instead he smiled
a lean,
mean
smile.

Small Hippo moved closer to Big Rhino.
"That smile scares me!"
he said.
"Don't worry,"
said Big Rhino.
"I will take care of you.
That's what big friends
are for!"

"Oh, dear," said Small Hippo.
"He's licking my big toe."

"Just kick up a bit,"
  said Big Rhino.

"Oh me oh my," said Small Hippo.
"Now he's munching on my tail."

"Just stick out your tongue at him,"
  said Big Rhino.

"Oh, no no NO!" cried Small Hippo.
"Now he's nibbling on my ear!"

"I think we'd better get out of here!"
said Big Rhino.
And they did.

But so did the alligator.
He got in front of Big Rhino
and Small Hippo
and blocked their way.

"What's the big hurry?"
he asked.
"Stay and play a game with me.
I have some riddles to ask you.
All you have to do is guess
the right answer."

"And if we can't?"
asked Small Hippo.
"What will happen then?"

The alligator smiled a lean, mean smile.
Then he opened his jaws wide
and went SNAP!

"Oh no!" cried Small Hippo.
"That's awful!"

"Don't worry, Small Hippo,"
  said Big Rhino.
"I am very good at riddles.
  I will answer for the two of us.
  That's what big friends are for."

"Ready?" asked the alligator.

"Whenever you are," said Big Rhino.

"Here goes," said the alligator.
"**What runs but cannot
walk downhill?**"

"Oh, that's easy," said Big Rhino.
"I know the answer to that one."

Big Rhino thought and thought some more.
"Don't tell me," he said.
"NEVER tell me 'cause I know
   the answer!"

The alligator smiled a lean, mean smile.
"Does that mean you give up?"

Big Rhino sighed.

"I really had the answer on the

tip of my tongue . . . .

But it got away.

So tell me.

What runs but cannot

walk downhill?"

The alligator licked his lips.

"Wait!" cried Small Hippo.
"I think I know the answer!"

"You do?" said the alligator.
"What is it?
   And you'd better be careful
   about what you say.
   **What runs but cannot
   walk downhill?**"

"Is it . . . Is it . . .

Water?" asked Small Hippo.

The alligator gave him a nasty look.
"It is," he said.

"But here's another one and it's even harder."

Alligator turned to Big Rhino.
"Here is the next riddle.
**What did King Arthur say
to his court?**"

Big Rhino pulled out
the thinking cap that
he happened to have with him.
He put it on and
he thought.
He thought very hard.
Very, very hard.
But it didn't do any good.

"Can't we play Monopoly?" he asked.
"Or capitals of countries?
 Or checkers, instead?"

"Time's up!" said the alligator.

And he pulled out some salt and pepper
that HE happened to have with him.

"Hold on!" cried Small Hippo.
"I think I know the answer to
**What did King Arthur say
to his court?**
The answer is . . .

**I want you all to go to
knight school!**"

The alligator kicked the ground.
"That's right," he said.
"But you're not finished yet."

The alligator moved closer to Big Rhino.
"Now here is the last riddle.
Remember!
You MUST answer it correctly.
If you don't . . .
anything can happen.
ANYTHING!

**What is always broken
before it is used?"**

Big Rhino sat down on a rock.
"I think better when I'm sitting,"
he said.

Then he thought and he thought
some more. His shoulders drooped.

"Ready to quit?" asked the alligator.

"I am," said Big Rhino.

"I know the answer," said Small Hippo.
"It's . . .

. . . It's **an egg!**"

The alligator gnashed his teeth.
But then he smiled his lean, mean smile.
"Perfect score for you, Small Hippo.
You may go free.
But Big Rhino didn't answer any
of the riddles.
So that means I get to eat him up!"

Big Rhino groaned.

But Small Hippo thought fast.

"Let's play a game for double or nothing,"
he said.

"I will give you a word puzzle to solve.
If you give the right answer . . ."
Small Hippo gulped.

The alligator's eyes lit up.
"I get to eat the two of you up,
instead of just one?" he asked.
"Is that what you mean by double
or nothing?"

"Exactly," said Small Hippo.

"And if I don't . . .?"

"Then we both go free," said Small Hippo.

The alligator thought for a minute.

Should he settle for one?

After all, one animal in the pot

IS worth two who are not!

On the other hand . . .

TWO would be a REAL treat!

"Okay," he said. "Let's play."

CUL8R ALLIGATOR

Small Hippo found a stick.

He wrote his word puzzle in the dirt.

CUL8R ALLIGATOR

"What does that say?"

he asked the alligator.

The alligator looked at the ground.

"Ha, ha, ha, that's easy," he said.

"Now let me see . . .

Oh, hi-dee-dee, oh, hi-dee-ho.

CUL8R ALLIGATOR

Hmmmm...

CUL8R AL

Hmmmm...

CUL8R ALLIGATOR

Hmmmm...

CUL8R ALLIGATOR

Oh, that's so easy.
Who wants to answer such a
stupid puzzle anyhow."

Without saying goodbye—
the alligator slid back into the water.

"He can't answer it,"
  said Small Hippo.
"Neither can I," said Big Rhino.
"What does it say?"

"It says, **See you later, Alligator,**"
  said Small Hippo.

"Not if I can help it," said Big Rhino.
  And he laughed.
  Then he said, "Now let's get out of here."

As they walked along the forest path,
Big Rhino put his arm
around Small Hippo.
"And may I say that small friends
can be as much help to big friends
as big friends are to small friends?"

"You may," said Small Hippo.
And he put his arm around Big Rhino.

Then together,
they set out to find
a different river to splash in.